I AM BRILLIANT!

Congratulations to graduates everywhere!
You are on your way!
—KH

To Gunnar,
a future kindergarten grad!
Love, Great Aunt Debbie xo

To my mom, who taught me with her example
that kindness is the best quality anyone can have.
—ARS

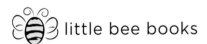 little bee books

New York, NY
Text copyright © 2021 by Kathryn Heling and Deborah Hembrook
Illustrations copyright © 2021 by Addy Rivera Sonda
Manufactured in China TPL 1120
littlebeebooks.com
First Edition
10 9 8 7 6 5 4 3 2 1
Library of Congress Cataloging-in-Publication Data is available upon request.
ISBN 978-1-4998-1065-3
For more information about special discounts on bulk purchases,
please contact Little Bee Books at sales@littlebeebooks.com.

GRADUATION GROOVE

by Kathryn Heling and Deborah Hembrook

illustrated by Addy Rivera Sonda

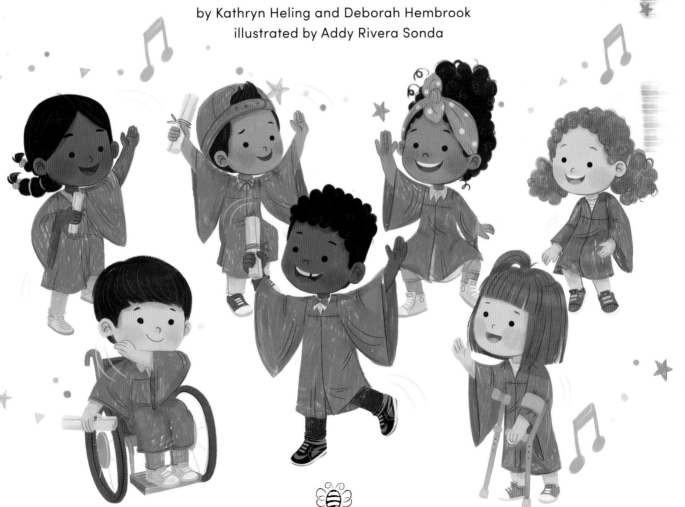

little bee books

Got the graduation groove
in my kindergarten feet.
I'm zipping up my gown
to a first-grade beat.

Got the graduation groove
on my kindergarten face.
Look how much I've grown!
I'm on first-grade pace.

Got the graduation groove
in my kindergarten hands.
I'm putting on my cap,
making first-grade plans.

Got the graduation groove
in my kindergarten head.

I'm in the bus, on my way,
first grade is just ahead.

Got the graduation groove
in my kindergarten brain.
I've got myself a seat
on the first-grade train.

Got the graduation groove
in my kindergarten heart.
Know my letters and my numbers,
feeling first-grade smart.

Got the graduation groove
in my kindergarten smile,
posing for the camera,
showing first-grade style.

Got the graduation groove
in my kindergarten knees.
I'm waiting on the stage
when suddenly . . . I FREEZE.

Got the first-grade jitters
in my kindergarten skin.
What if I don't like it?
My insides start to spin.

I'll really miss our hamster
and projects that we made.
What about my teacher?
Can SHE come to first grade?

But then I see my grandma
and spot my mom and dad.
I hear my name announced—
I'm a kindergarten grad!

Listen! Hear the music?
The cheering, clapping crowd?
I've crossed the stage, bowed, and waved.
I'm feeling first-grade proud.

Got the graduation groove
in my kindergarten hips.

Holding my diploma,
doing first-grade flips!

There's a graduation party
with cupcakes and high fives.
Kindergarten's over,
time for end-of-year goodbyes.

Got the graduation groove
with my kindergarten friends.
We'll have a first-grade beat
when the celebration ends.

Kindergarten was awesome,
but first grade, here we come!
New classroom and new teacher,
new ways to have fun!

When summer days are over
and school begins once more,
I'll grab my brand-new backpack
and dance on through the door!

I've got a first-grade groove
and I'm feeling supercool.
The bus is here—off I go!
I'm on my way to school!